Fitting In

Jada Jones

Bein' Good

Blind Trust

Fitting In

Holding Back

Keepin' Her Man

www.sdlback.com

ISBN-13: 978-1-61651-777-9
ISBN-10: 1-61651-777-8
eBook: 978-1-61247-339-0

Printed in Guangzhou, China
1111/CA21101798

16 15 14 13 12   1 2 3 4 5

[chapter]

1

The cafeteria was empty. Tia Ramirez ran her hand through her long, brown hair. She looked around again. Tia couldn't be wrong, could she?

The sign in the main school hallway had said:

> **Yearbook Club Meeting—**
> Join Today! Make Memories
> and Friends for a Lifetime!
> Meet in the Cafeteria Monday
> after School. Let's Make This
> the BEST Yearbook Ever!

It seemed clear. Tia read the sign three times. She was in the right place for sure.

She really wanted to join yearbook club. Before her family left Mexico, she had read about the clubs American schools had. This one sounded like the most fun.

But no one was there. Tia headed back toward the cafeteria doors. She must have read something wrong. Tia still had to work hard to understand English. She wasn't going to let it stop her from getting what she wanted, though. She'd even joined the debate team as a way to improve her English. Practicing speeches for debate might not be the easiest way to get better, but Tia was up for the challenge. Yearbook would be another challenge that Tia wasn't going to give up on. If she had to read that yearbook club sign one hundred times to get it right, she'd do it.

Tia reached for the door, but it flew open in her face. Her eyes opened wide. A group of chattering students passed her. Everyone was coming for yearbook club! A few said hi to Tia or gave her a wave. She'd got it right after all.

Tia watched about a dozen people spread out at the lunch tables. She knew who most of them were. Kiki Butler, the tomboy of her class, sat at a table with Misha and Tara. Tia also knew Kiki's twin sister, girlie-girl Sherise, and her sort of obnoxious sidekick, Marnyke. Sometimes Sherise and Marnyke could be nice. But often they were downright cruel.

Everyone was talking and messing around, waiting for the meeting to begin. Tia noticed there was no one else like her, no one else who spoke Spanish. She sighed. Almost a quarter of South Central High struggled with English. Not one other immigrant student wanted to be in the yearbook club? She didn't understand why. Tia thought everyone

———

should be in at least one club. That was the way to get ahead.

Marnyke and Sherise sat down near where Tia was still standing. Tia could feel Sherise's eyes look her up and down. "Yo, Marnyke. Looks like someone is lost."

"Probably can't read the signs. Think she's lookin' for an English tutor or somethin'?" Marnyke smirked.

Sherise laughed. "Yeah, *someone* can't speak English very good. Did you hear her in class today? She didn't seem to know what class she was in. She didn't even know the word *chemistry*."

Tia couldn't listen any more. Sherise was being mean because Tia had pointed out all the wrong answers on Sherise's history assignment last week. Before that, they'd hung out a lot. Now Sherise was making fun of Tia every chance she got.

Tia sat down at a table in the back by herself. She pulled out a notebook. "If I look busy, maybe they will knock it off. I just want them to leave me alone," Tia thought.

The other students seemed oblivious to what was going on. They didn't even look over at Tia. She could see Jackson Beauford, the biggest player at school. He was in her math class. Jackson was the one who ignored her when she asked him for some extra paper last week. His bright blue eyes had looked right through her. Tia never felt so stupid in her whole life.

Jackson was hanging around with Darnell Watson, the star jock of the school. Darnell was Tia's friend these days. They ate lunch together sometimes. Darnell even asked her for help with his Spanish homework. They'd meet after school or when basketball practice was over so she could work with him. He didn't seem to have a problem with her.

Or at least not when it was just the two of them.

Tia knew Darnell was hot stuff at school. Everyone always bragged how his jump shot just might land him on a pro basketball team someday. They also gossiped about his shady side. There were rumors he was still involved with gangs. Tia didn't believe one word of it. Darnell was always really sweet to Tia.

Tia watched Marnyke pull down her already low-cut, tight tank top. Sherise proceeded to brush out her hair, drawing as much attention to herself as possible. Then Marnyke and Sherise went over to where the boys had taken over a table. Tia shook her head in disgust. Those girls had only one thing on their minds. And it sure wasn't yearbook club.

"Hey, girlfriend," someone said from above Tia's head. She looked up. The voice had come from a slightly bigger girl with curly brown hair. It was Nishell Saunders. Nishell had been one of the first people to introduce herself to Tia on her first day of school. Tia liked her immediately. Nishell was always so friendly and outgoing. She couldn't care less what others thought. And Nishell didn't seem to be bothered by Tia's obvious accent. Or anything else.

"This the meetin' for the yearbook club?" Nishell asked.

Tia nodded happily. She was glad Nishell was talking to her. A lot of people either ignored Tia or made fun of her. Like Marnyke and Sherise.

"Cool," Nishell said with a smile. She plopped down next to Tia. She looked around. "Looks like we're all by ourselves over here, huh? Why didn't you sit with Marnyke and Sherise, home girl?"

Tia shrugged. Tia knew Nishell liked to hang with popular, pretty girls like

Marnyke. But why did Tia have to hang with them too? Was hanging out with Tia not enough for Nishell?

"I just didn't," Tia told her.

Tia waited for her to get up and move to hang with the cool crowd. Suddenly, they heard a loud whistle.

"Attention everyone!"

Tia turned around to see that a woman had just come into the room. She made the high-pitched whistle with her fingers again. Everybody quieted down.

"I'm Ms. Okoro for those of you who don't know me. Most students call me Ms. O," she said. Ms. Okoro seemed really excited. She was smiling and talking really fast. She had an accent too. Tia leaned forward to try to understand her better.

"Welcome to our first yearbook club meeting. I can't wait for us to get started! I know we're a small group right now, but there is much we can accomplish this year. I hope you all will have fun and work hard too. First off, some quick business. We'll be meeting most days after school. Members are expected to attend at least three meetings a week. Last year's yearbook never did get finished and ..."

Ms. Okoro trailed off. She was looking at Darnell's raised hand. Her lips thinned.

"Yes, Mr. Watson? Question?" she asked.

"Three days a week!" exclaimed Darnell. "Last year, Mr. Thompson only had meetings once every two weeks. No offense or nothin'."

Ms. Okoro frowned. "I am aware of how Mr. Thompson ran the yearbook club. I am also aware that he and Mr. Crandall established joining yearbook club as a way for students to make up for their bad behavior. If you are here for that reason, you are still expected to actually participate all year. That's if you want me to sign your release form to show you completed the work to get out of detention."

Loud groans came from the group. Tia was curious. The yearbook club was something she'd been interested in since she got to South Central High. She was *so* looking forward to this meeting. "Were most of the others really only here to get out of trouble?" Tia wondered.

That certainly seemed to be the case for Marnyke and Darnell. They were making the most noise about having to come to so many meetings.

Tia heard Marnyke complain, "For real? Three nights a week? Hell, I ain't got that kinda time. I got way more important things to do with my life!"

"Yeah. I hear ya. That's a load of crap! I gotta work besides, ya know," Sherise said.

Tia noticed that Nishell didn't make a peep. "Maybe Nishell is here because she wants to be here too," Tia thought.

Ms. Okoro kept talking. She ignored the grumbling. "Come on, guys. This is the year to make the yearbook club fun and cool. We can turn this club around! This year, we'll have more student direction. In addition to actually creating a yearbook, we can make the club something to be proud of!

"A week from today, you're going to vote for a yearbook club president. This will be an important role. We'll show the school we are not just a club for troublemakers."

Everyone in the room looked at each other in shock. Yearbook club president? That sounded so real. And not fun. Sherise raised her hand.

"Is the president, like, gonna be in charge of all the fun stuff too? Like parties, maybe school dances, picking pictures, and bringing treats?"

Tia rolled her eyes. This wasn't supposed to be a popularity contest. It was serious work. Commitment. Dedication. Stuff Sherise wouldn't know if it smacked her in the face.

"Yes, that's part of it, Sherise. This person will be the spokesperson for the yearbook club. He or she will talk at assemblies and work with the student council. But it will also be up to this person to make sure the yearbook gets finished. It should be somebody who is responsible and cares about the yearbook club. And who can help everyone find a way to make the best yearbook ever. We can be a team," Ms. Okoro said.

Tia sat up straighter in her seat. She could see herself as the president. If anyone could make sure the yearbook got out, she could.

Ms. Okoro continued, "If you want to run for president, let me know by Wednesday. You'll need to write an election speech. Speeches should be ready by Friday morning so I can review them. The candidates will give their speeches at Friday's meeting, and you'll all vote on Monday. It might be worth trying to get some other friends to join this week. It could mean extra votes for you.

"Okay, enough business. Let's get to some fun! I want you to break into smaller groups. Introduce yourselves to each other. Tell each other about your favorite things to do. And talk about what you're most jazzed to do in yearbook club this year."

Tia forgot about being president for the moment. There were other things to worry about now. Would anyone want to partner with her? Tia started chewing her fingernails. What if she was left alone?

Nishell was looking around. She waved to someone across the room. "Great. Any minute Nishell will get up and leave me sitting alone. As usual," Tia thought.

Nishell turned to Tia. "Hey, can Misha join us? She's super slick."

Tia smiled. Maybe she wouldn't be alone after all! "Sure," she said.

Misha sat down and Nishell instantly took over. She acted like she was meeting both girls for the first time.

"So, I'm Nishell. I love art, especially photography. I wanna be a famous photographer. And I wanna take all the pictures for the yearbook. I got this great new camera. It's better than the school's. The photos are gonna be way cooler than last year. Even though no one ever saw them."

"Baller!" Misha said next. "I'm Misha, and my favorite subject is history. My grandpa's workin' on a family history book. Kinda like a family tree, ya know? I thought workin' on the yearbook might be a way to learn how to put together all the stuff he's got."

"What 'bout you, home girl?" Nishell asked Tia.

Tia wanted to tell them how she thought the yearbook club would be a great way to succeed in school and make friends. And how she wanted to keep memories of this year at South Central High. But before Tia could say a word, she was rudely cut off.

"Hey, girls!" Sherise bounded over. "Let's get down to it. Why did y'all join YC?"

Misha, Tia, and Nishell looked at each other. Sherise was staring at Tia. Why was Sherise in her face?

"YC?" Tia asked shyly. She hadn't heard this before.

"YC? It's, like, ah, short for yearbook club. Duh. I thought *everyone* knew that." Sherise rolled her eyes.

Tia wanted to hide under the table.

"Hey, step off, Sherise. I bet Tia knows tons of words you don't. 'Specially since you're already failing Spanish," Nishell said.

Sherise glared at Nishell. "What's up your butt? I was just tryin' to be nice," Sherise said and walked off. Tia was so glad Nishell came to her defense. She could tell they were going to be friends.

"Girl needs to chill. Did you see her tryin' to get up in everybody's business?" Nishell shrugged.

Misha nodded. "It's like she's always gotta be the queen bee. Wanna bet she runs for president? She'd be a good one too."

Tia didn't think Sherise would be a good president at all. It would take too

18

much hard work. But Sherise sure knew how to get attention. She acted like she was everyone's best friend! She only shut up when Ms. O told her to let some of the others speak.

The meeting ended. Sherise high-fived or hugged everyone and gave them flirty smiles and winks. "What a poser Sherise is," Tia thought.

"*Adios*," Sherise said to Tia with a smirk. Then Sherise left with Marnyke, and everyone just followed her. Unbelievable.

Why was Sherise trying to rag on Tia? To make her feel bad? Tia wasn't going to let Sherise walk all over her. She wasn't going to let Sherise win.

Knead and roll. Knead and roll. Add more flour. Repeat.

The words ran through Tia's head as she mixed the bread dough. It was hard work. It took dedication and a lot of attention to make it just right. Tia could hear her Grandmama Alma teaching her in Spanish. Tia learned everything she knew about making bread from her grandmama. And a lot about life too.

Tia brushed her hair out of her eyes with her arm. Her hands were full of flour. Across the room in the big window, the sky was starting to turn pink. The sun was coming up. Finally. Tia had been working since 5:00 a.m. The bakery, Pasteles Bonitas, was her family's business.

"Hola, hija. Cómo estás?" asked Tia's mama, Carlota. *Hello, daughter. How are you?* Tia's family spoke Spanish to each other most of the time. It was easier. Carlota said it was their native language. Why should they lose their heritage? But she did not understand it made life harder for Tia. Tia wanted to learn English better. She wanted to fit in so people wouldn't make fun of her at school so much.

Tia shrugged. "Okay," she said.

"Mi hija!" Carlota exclaimed. "What's wrong? You don't seem like yourself."

"I don't want to go to school today," Tia said.

"Why not?" Carlota asked. "You love school. You are always the best in your class."

Tia sighed. "I don't understand what other people say or mean sometimes. I'm even having a hard time in science."

"That can't be," Carlota said as she rolled out the *churro* dough. Later it would be deep-fried and covered in sugar and cinnamon. *Churros* were Tia's favorite thing to eat with hot chocolate. The bakery was known all around the neighborhood for their delicious pastries.

Tia could feel her mama waiting for Tia to answer. Carlota was a strong-willed woman. She and Manuel, Tia's *papi*, came to America with enough money to start their own bakery. "All things come with patience and the will to do good," Carlota would always say.

"It's just school," Tia huffed after a few seconds. "Mama, kids make fun of my accent. And nobody understands what I try to say. Even when I speak *inglés*."

"Ah, but you were the best in your English class!" Carlota replied.

"Mama, no one here cares." Tia frowned. "Even the teachers think I'm dumb. I work hard, but when I got a perfect score on the math quiz last week, the teacher asked if I cheated!"

Carlota shook her head. "No child of mine would ever cheat."

"I know, Mama!" Tia exclaimed. "I didn't. I asked Mrs. Lister who she thought I copied. I was the only one who had all the answers right. Now, everyone tries to cheat off me!"

Carlota gave Tia a small smile. "You make us proud."

"I don't feel proud, Mama," Tia said. "Not when the girls say terrible things behind my back. Most of the boys don't talk to me either."

"Don't take any notice of them," Carlota said.

Tia sighed. "It's not easy. There are these two girls. They are so mean. They make jokes about me. They think I don't understand."

"Tia, *mi corazón*," Carlota said. "You cannot let fools get to you. You are better than that. You just have to stand up to them. Then they'll leave you alone."

Tia shook her head. A week ago she would have agreed with her mama, but now, after everyone had been mean to her? Could her mama even understand that girls like Marnyke and Sherise turn their backs on you in an instant? They played everyone. Tia kept kneading the dough. It was almost time to go to school. Tia could tell she was not getting out of it.

"There are cruel girls everywhere. Maybe they are just afraid. Afraid everyone will see through them. Be strong. Stand your ground. They will see they can't mess with you," Carlota said.

"I don't feel very tough, Mama," Tia said. She didn't feel like herself at all. Tia knew she was usually upbeat and optimistic. After everything that happened yesterday at the YC meeting though, it was hard.

Tia looked over at her little brother. Tomás was yawning and kneading his own dough with Manuel. Tomás smiled and waved a floured hand at Tia. Tomás really looked up to Tia.

"He's learning English faster than your *papi* is!" Carlota said proudly. "Tomás loves working with his hands too. He wants to be just like you. Someone is counting on you to lead the way. "

Tia smiled. She worked with Tomás on his English. It was the least she could do. When he went to school next year, he'd know every word. Tia couldn't bear to think of her brother getting teased like she was.

"I just don't want my life anymore." Tia knew that was a horrible thing to say. She pounded on the dough. At least she could take it out on something.

Carlota took Tia's hands away from the dough and held them. "I know that's not true," she said. "I can see it's hard. School is just starting. You will do fine. You have friends and will make more. Remember, smarts will get you where you want to go. I know you are strong, *mi hija.*"

"Mama is right. Why am I being such a wimp?" Tia thought. She straightened up. Her downer mood turned positive. "Mama, I'm going to run for president," Tia announced. Carlota's eyebrows went up. "Yearbook club president," Tia explained.

Tia surprised herself. She had been daydreaming about running. But Tia hadn't really decided until it came out of her mouth. Now that she had said it, she knew, deep down, that she wanted to be YC president more than anything.

"This is the first I've heard of this. Why?" her mama asked. Carlota still seemed surprised considering the talk they were just having.

"Because," Tia said, "being YC president is a perfect chance to show everyone what we Latinas can do. I'd be helping organize school events. That's in addition to making sure the yearbook gets out this year. I would work with everyone and show them I'm just as good as they are."

"Are you sure?" Carlota asked. "It sounds like a lot of work."

"*Si*," Tia said. Ready or not, she was running. "Yes, it'll take a lot of work. But I know I can do it. It will be good for me."

Carlota gave her a hug. "It sounds like you've got the right attitude and spirit!"

Tia smiled and hugged her back. She felt like she was halfway to winning!

Then she saw the clock over Carlota's head. Tia gasped. If she didn't leave now, she'd be late for school. Tia's phone buzzed in her pocket. But she had no time to look at it.

"Mama, I gotta go. I'll be late!" She quickly washed her hands and grabbed her backpack. "*Gracias*. Thanks for all the help!" she said, blowing a kiss to her mama as she ran out the door.

Tia was flying high. Even having to run the five blocks to the bus stop couldn't bring her down. Tia would be a great yearbook club president. When she won, even Marnyke and Sherise would think she was cool.

Tia wasn't worried about competition. Almost everyone at the meeting yesterday was there to get out of detention, not because they wanted to be in YC. Being president would be a lot of work. Tia wanted to take it on, but she knew it wasn't for everybody.

At the bus stop, Tia's phone buzzed again. There were two messages from Kiki. The first one said, "Chica where r u?"

The next one was, "Big news. Get here fast. C u asap."

Tia wondered what was up already. It was early in the day. Besides, Tia had some big news of her own.

The bus arrived and Tia hopped on. She quickly found an empty seat and texted Kiki back, "On the bus. B there soon."

Then her thoughts jumped to the speech. To run for yearbook club president, Tia would have to give a speech in front of everyone in YC. In English. Tia gulped. She got nervous just trying to speak to one person smoothly.

Some people had trouble, or pretended to have trouble, understanding Tia when she spoke. Would that be a reason, or excuse, for people not to vote for her?

Tia chewed on her nails and looked out the bus window. What would she do? Tia needed help. That was for sure. Tia and Kiki got along pretty well. And Kiki was a good student. Kiki was Tia's best chance to win. Tia spent the rest of the ride planning on how to ask Kiki for her help.

Tia felt on top of the world again. Once Kiki said yes, nothing could stop Tia from becoming YC president. Tia was sure of it.

[chapter]

3

Tia could hardly sit still the rest of the way to school. She thought about what she needed to do when she got there. First, Tia had to find Kiki and tell her she had decided to run for YC president. And Tia really needed Kiki to help her with her speech. Maybe she should just text Kiki to give her a heads-up. No, no time. The bus stopped. Tia flew off.

Tia ran up the steps into school and grabbed some books from her locker. Then she bolted to Kiki's locker.

It was ten minutes before the bell. She sent Kiki a text, "Kiki where r u?"

Tia danced with impatience. She just couldn't stand still.

"Hey, girl. I knew you was smart. But damn, I ain't never seen nobody that excited for first period to start." It was Jackson. He was opening the locker next to Kiki's. Was he talking to her? Tia looked over her shoulder to make sure.

"I ... I'm not. I just need to ask Kiki a question," Tia told Jackson.

"Got it. Girl stuff." Jackson winked. "I'll keep it *en secret-o*." Was Jackson making fun of her, or trying to be nice?

Tia smiled, unsure. "Actually, it's about YC," Tia said.

Jackson made a face. "Girl, YC is whack," he said. "I jus' go to keep crusty Mr. Crandall off my back."

"I heard that, Mr. Beauford." A stern voice came from behind Jackson. Jackson jumped and turned around. It was Principal Olson!

"That is no way to refer to our guidance counselor. Mr. Crandall is a respected member of our faculty. That comment gets you a week of detention, young man," Mr. Olson said.

Tia shook her head. She didn't like Mr. Crandall either. But even she knew better than to call him names when the principal or any teachers were around.

"You too, young lady," Mr. Olson continued. "You've got a week of detention as well."

Tia's mouth dropped. She hadn't even done anything!

"Don't play dumb with me," Mr. Olson warned. "I saw that look." He gave them each a detention slip and walked away.

Tia couldn't believe what had just happened. Jackson grinned. "Never got one of these before, huh?" he said.

"This is all your fault!" Tia was furious. She'd never gotten detention before.

Sherise and Kiki appeared from around the corner. They were with another senior, Ty Kessler. Ty was Tia's biggest crush. He was tall, cool, and he even spoke some Spanish. Once in a while he came into the bakery. He'd wait until Tia was free and place his order with her. Tia felt herself starting to sweat. She didn't want anyone knowing she had detention. Especially Ty.

"Who's what's fault? Spill. Now!" Sherise demanded.

"No-thing. It's, ah, not a thing," Tia muttered. She stuffed the pink slip into her pocket.

Jackson laughed. "Mr. Olson snuck up on us. We got detention this week, me and Tia. Don't we? Her first time too, if you know what I mean."

"Aw, man!" Ty said. "I woulda loved to been 'round for that! Detention ain't no thang, girl. It'd be a piece a cake if I had

34

it with you, Tia." Ty smiled at her. Tia felt her cheeks get hot.

"Damn straight. I'm actually excited for detention now." Jackson winked at Tia again before closing his locker. "See ya 'round, *chi-cas*."

Jackson and Ty walked off into the crowd. After they left, Sherise turned to Tia. "Gettin' detention? And flirtin' with Jackson? You're livin' dangerously, girl! Just be careful, 'cause you know Jackson plays everybody."

Tia was confused. Getting detention because she was standing next to Jackson counted as flirting? Tia had hoped Ty was flirting with her instead! Before Tia could reply, Kiki walked right up next to Tia. She saved Tia from total embarrassment.

Kiki rolled her eyes. "You don't need to be dissin' Tia 'bout no guy, sis. Don't be jumpin' down her throat."

"Yeah, right," Sherise said. She backed off. "You ain't his type anyways."

Tia didn't have time for this. Ty was the guy she really wanted. But even that wasn't important right now. She needed to talk to Kiki about YC. She ignored Sherise and spoke to Kiki.

"Kiki, I have to ask you something. Fast," she said.

"Excuse me. I am still in the conversation! I have something real important to say too." Sherise pushed Tia.

"Chill out." Kiki slammed her locker. "Reesie, we been talkin' all mornin' about Jackson and Darnell. And you wouldn't shut up to Ty about your boy Carlos. What more could you have to say? Can't you just give Tia a minute?"

Sherise stood up straight. "No, this is something *real* important. Everybody is gonna know soon."

"Then spit it out!" Kiki told her.

"I've decided to run for YC president," Sherise announced loudly.

"What do you mean? I'm running for YC president!" Tia exclaimed.

"Since when have you ever wanted to put that kinda work into anything, Reesie?" Kiki asked.

"Like Ms. O said, YC needs a leader. Well, guess what? *I'm* a born leader."

"No, YC needs someone who will work hard and really wants to do it," Tia said.

"They need me," Sherise insisted. She got right in Tia's face. "Someone who can com-mun-i-cate with ev-ery-one."

Tia's eyes narrowed. It was time to stand up for herself. "I can com-mun-i-cate just fine. Watch me." It was Tia's turn to get in Sherise's face. "Sherise, there's a word for *chicas* like you. They're called—"

"Okay, home girls, chill out." Kiki stepped squarely between them. "Looks like we got enough debate goin' on here already."

Tia stepped back. She was done letting people walk all over her. Maybe now Sherise would leave Tia alone for good. But Tia was dreaming.

Sherise snapped back. She always got the last word. "Well, it's not even about the work anyway." Sherise tossed her hair and put her hand on her hip. "It's about who gets the most votes. And there ain't no beatin' me at that, girl."

Sherise whirled around. She walked up to Darnell who was passing by in the hallway. "Say, Darnell. Give me a little love. I can always count on your vote for YC president. Right, sugar?" Sherise asked, batting her eyelashes.

Darnell just shook his head and kept walking. "Hey, boy. 'Member our little meetin' by your locker last week? You best vote for me if you want more where that came from," Tia heard Sherise yell at Darnell. He disappeared quickly.

Kiki shook her head. "I can't believe that girl. She can get real crazy sometimes."

Tia shook her head. "I just don't get her. Why she gotta pick a fight?"

Kiki shrugged. "Looks like running for YC president might be a pretty big battle to pick."

"I just want to make YC the best club ever, you know?" Tia said.

Kiki shrugged. "I know. I actually think you'd be a better president than Sherise."

"Really?" Tia smiled. She started to feel a little more up again. Maybe Kiki would help her after all. "You mean it?"

"Don't tell Sherise I said that, though," Kiki said.

Tia felt her shoulders sink. "You texted me about big news. What is it?" Tia asked.

"It was just 'bout Sherise running for YC president. But that's old news now, since you know," Kiki replied.

"Well, I decided to run for YC president before I knew about Sherise. I told my mama this morning. Will you help me with my speech?" Tia asked bravely.

Kiki's eyes widened. She looked upset.

"Kiki, you're the only one I can think of who can really help me," Tia said.

Kiki looked at her feet. "I don't know, Tia. I mean, I woulda said yes for sure. But with Sherise also runnin', I dunno."

"Please?" Tia pleaded. "I won't care if you help Sherise too."

Kiki snorted. "I don't think Reesie will ask me for help with anythin'. But she's family. I gotta respect that. Sorry, I don't think I can." Tia could see Kiki felt bad, but she still needed help with her speech.

Tia tried not to cry. What was she going to do now?

The one-minute bell rang, and she and Kiki ran to their first class together. People were laughing and joking up and down the hallway. But Kiki and Tia were silent.

Tia plopped down in her seat just as the tardy bell rang. She was disappointed. What if Kiki wouldn't help her? Would they still be friends? Could Tia be friends with Kiki if she sided with Sherise? "It's not like Sherise even cares about YC. She just wants to win," Tia thought.

Tia was in her own little world. She had been feeling so good since the talk with her mama this morning. Now, Sherise was running for YC president against her, and Tia had to find someone other than Kiki to help her with her speech. And she had detention too! That was a lot to deal with the first hour of school.

Tia thought about dropping out of the race. But she'd already told Sherise and Kiki she was running. And by now they had probably texted the whole school. It would be Tia's worst nightmare if she backed out now. Sherise would only make her life more miserable. And what would her mama say?

Tia's stomach churned with each thought. Tia looked around the room. She felt like everyone turned away so they didn't have to look at her. Tia felt like she was having trouble breathing.

"What do they know?" Tia wondered, her brain going round and round with questions. Were they judging her? Would running for YC president be one of the best decisions she'd ever made, or one of the worst?

All day, Tia felt eyes on her every move. She made sure to talk to everyone she knew. She asked them to join YC and vote for her. She wasn't going to let Sherise bring her down.

In fact, Tia was looking for a fight. She'd go and show up Sherise, who was probably holding court in the lunch-room right now. Tia just had to make sure she looked her best. She applied another coat of lip gloss, and then shut her locker.

"*Hola, chica!*" It was Ty again. He was so cute. She just wanted to melt.

"What you doin', girl? I ain't seen you in forever." He leaned against the locker next to Tia's.

Ty always made Tia's heart beat faster. He'd text Tia sometimes, just to ask what was up. Last week, when he came into the bakery, he'd flirted with Tia too much. Her mom had noticed and wasn't happy. Tia avoided Ty for a while, but now here he was, looking her up!

"Hey, Ty!" Tia said. She couldn't think of what else to say. "What are you doing here?"

Ty shrugged. He ran a hand over his shaved head. "Needed a walk around the school. Felt like I was bein' smothered by Sherise in the cafeteria." Ty mimicked Sherise's high-pitched girlie voice, "'Join YC! Darnell and Jackson are in it. Why ain't you?'" He switched back to a normal voice, "Darnell and Jackson are way cool, but I ain't stupid enough to get stuck in some dumbass club like YC. So why you over here?"

Tia blushed. Ty thought YC was stupid? Would he find out from someone that Tia was running for yearbook club president? Would he think Tia was stupid too?

"This is my locker. I'm just getting ready," Tia told him.

"Getting ready for what? Askin' some other guy out on a date?" Ty asked with a smile.

Tia shook her head. "I'm not going on a date," Tia said. She didn't want to talk about YC and have Ty make fun of her.

"Well, I guess I shouldn't be complainin'. If you ain't gettin' ready for another guy, just means I get you all to myself. Especially since I ain't seen you around lately." He leaned in closer to Tia.

"Oh, yeah?" Tia asked. "And why would you want that?"

"Well ..." Ty grabbed Tia's hand. Tia felt her heart pounding out of her chest. Was Ty about to tell her he liked her? Would he ask her out?

BRRRRRRRRING!

Tia and Ty both jumped. It was the bell! Lunch was over. Before Tia could say anything else, the halls were flooded with people.

Ty quickly let go of Tia's hand and backed away. It was like they weren't even standing together! After Ty said "Hey" to a few guys, he didn't even look over at Tia. She felt angry at his apparent snub. Ty would flirt with her when they were alone but not when other people were around? He thought YC was a joke too! Tia decided he really wasn't worth her time. What did they even have in common?

"See ya later, Ty!" Tia yelled at him furiously. She started walking away.

"Tia, wait!" Ty called. He rushed to catch up with her. "Lemme walk you to class."

Tia nodded, but she was still mad and hurt. "What was the point?" she thought.

"What are you doin' later, Tia?" Ty asked. "I was thinkin' we could get pizza or somethin'."

Ten minutes ago, Tia would have jumped all over the chance. Now she knew she had to tell Ty the truth. She didn't want to step out with anyone who thought the things she loved, the things she worked for, were dumb. And she really didn't want him to dis her to his friends.

Tia stayed quiet until they got to the door of her class. "I'm in YC too." She told him. "And I'm running for club president. Just thought you should know I'm a dumbass like the rest of them. Guess you're just too cool for me, right?"

—

47

She went into the classroom and let the door shut behind her. Right in his face.

Tia heard whispering in front of her. She saw Marnyke and Sherise giggling and passing notes.

Tia tried not to pay attention. "There's no reason to think they're talking about me," Tia thought. Then Sherise looked right at her, laughed, and turned around. Tia clenched her teeth. Did they see what had happened with Ty? Did they know how humiliated Tia was?

"Hey, Tia." Darnell sat down in the desk next to her. "How's it goin'?"

"It's baller," Tia lied. Darnell had told her last week during their tutoring session that *baller* meant *cool*. She helped him with Spanish. He helped her with English.

Darnell grinned at her. "Dang, girl. You got it!"

Darnell always made her feel good. Lots of people thought he was bad news. But he was always nice to Tia.

Tia smiled at Darnell. She was glad he was in this class with her. She wished she could tell him about what happened with Ty, but she didn't want certain others hearing. Tia saw Marnyke and Sherise pass another note. Marnyke looked back at Tia and Darnell. Marnyke told everyone Darnell was her man. Never mind Sherise was flirting with him behind Marnyke's back, though.

Tia played it cool. She pretended not to notice Marnyke's frown. It was time to forget about Ty and remember her main goal. Becoming the YC president.

"Darnell, you goin' to the YC meeting?" Tia asked.

"Yeah," Darnell said. "I guess. Why?"

"Well, I'm running for YC president. I hope you'll vote for me," Tia said loudly.

Sherise whipped her head around to stare at Tia. She looked really agitated.

"That's real cool, Tia. You know somebody else is runnin' too, right?" Darnell said.

"I heard Sherise was going to, maybe," Tia muttered.

"Guess you'll have to win my vote then," Darnell joked.

"Win it?" Tia asked.

"Yeah, like, offer me stuff. Make promises you're not gonna keep," Darnell said.

Tia couldn't believe it. "People do that?"

Darnell laughed. "Don't you know about school elections? They are *da bomb!* People throwin' parties. Doin' favors. Handin' out 'candy,' if you know what I mean. They all talk about how legit they are and how lame everybody else is."

If the election was really like that, Tia wouldn't have a chance. Tia knew Sherise would be all over Darnell in a second. She would give him anything he wanted just so Darnell would vote for her instead of Tia. Plus, if Sherise got Darnell's vote, she'd get Jackson's. Jackson usually did whatever Darnell did.

Tia chewed on her already short fingernails. If Jackson voted for Sherise, who else would? Jackson could get all the other girls to vote the same way he did. Tia knew Nishell had a longtime crush on Jackson too. Tia could be left with no votes at all!

She spent the rest of class wondering what to do. Sherise was going to do whatever it took to win this election. Tia had to think of something to stop her. And fast.

Tia needed help. She couldn't ask Kiki again. Kiki said she wanted Tia to win. But Kiki wouldn't totally dis her sister.

Nishell was the only other YC member Tia knew who actually cared about the club. She and Tia were getting to be better friends. Maybe she would help Tia. Nishell hung out in the art room after school when she wasn't at YC. Mr. Gupta taught art. He was Nishell's favorite teacher. Tia liked him too.

Tia saw Nishell down the hallway in a corner. She was heading for Mr. Gupta's classroom.

"*Hola*, Nishell!" Tia waved. Nishell put her finger to her lips motioning for Tia to be quiet. Tia walked up to Nishell. "What's goin—"

Nishell reached over and covered Tia's mouth. "Shut up, okay?" Nishell whispered and pointed. They peeked around the corner.

Sherise was hanging all over Jackson. "That's one way to get votes," Tia thought.

———

Nishell yanked Tia back. "Careful! They'll see you," she said. Tia heard Sherise's laugh echo down the hallway.

"They are flirting, no?" Tia asked.

"*Si*. Now keep it down," Nishell said. Then Nishell snapped a picture of Sherise and Jackson on her phone.

"Let's interrupt their little meeting," Tia suggested in a whisper.

"What? No!" Nishell straightened up. But Tia could tell she was still listening.

"Yes!" Tia was thinking fast. "*Vaya*! Go!" Tia pushed Nishell into the hallway.

Sherise and Jackson saw Nishell. They stepped apart awkwardly. "Oh, hey, guys," Tia heard Nishell say.

Then Jackson mumbled something. Tia heard footsteps and a door slam. Sherise rushed around the corner. She didn't even see Tia up against the wall. After a minute, Tia peeked around to see Nishell stomping toward her.

"What happened?" Tia asked.

"What *happened*?" Nishell spat. "Jackson walked away. He wouldn't even look at me. Then Sherise pretended like I didn't even exist! It was so embarrassing."

Tia didn't know what to say. "They are not flirting no more, though, right?"

"Yeah, but now they're not talkin' to me either. Thanks to you, Tia," Nishell said sarcastically.

Tia's heart sank. Pushing Nishell to stop Sherise from getting Jackson to vote for her was as bad as Sherise making out with him to get his vote. It was wrong. Tia knew from now on she'd have to get votes a different way.

"I'm so sorry, Nishell. It was not right. Pushing you."

"Damn straight!" Nishell swore.

"You like him," Tia said. "I just tried to make it right for you." She knew that wasn't the whole truth. But she couldn't bring herself to say that she used Nishell to get ahead in the YC race.

Nishell didn't seem so angry all of a sudden. "I know, Tia. Thanks for watchin' my back. I can't trust Sherise, even though we're supposed to be friends." Tia agreed but didn't say anything.

"That's why you gotta win that election," Nishell continued. "I don't want no two-timin' liar like Sherise callin' the shots at YC."

"Will you help me write my speech?" Tia asked.

"Totally. Let's do it!" Nishell said, high-fiving Tia. "Tell Ms. O you're in. Sherise already told her. It's game on, girl. We can start workin' on your speech in the art room after school."

Tia's day was finally looking up. Maybe she had a chance to beat Sherise after all.

—
[chapter]

5

Tia grabbed some books from her locker on the way to her next class. As she started down the hall, Tia saw Sherise and Ty.

She could hear Sherise telling him how she would be the best YC president ever. "I have attended South Central longer than the other candidate," Sherise said. Then she added snidely, "It should be like running for president of the United States. The candidates should have to be born in America.

"What a mean dig," Tia thought. She watched Ty's face. He didn't look happy, but he didn't say anything to correct Sherise either. When Ty saw Tia he smiled and tried to walk over to her. Tia shook her head and ran into the nearest bathroom.

She sent a text to Nishell to let her know what was going on. Tia felt terrible. She leaned over the sink. Tia was going to miss her next class. She didn't care. All Tia could hear were Sherise's words echoing in her head. All she could see was the way Ty just stood there, listening.

"Whaz up? where r u?" Nishell texted.

Tia texted her back. "Bathroom. I feel sick."

"C u in a sec," Nishell answered.

Tia took a deep breath. Nishell was on her way. Things would be better. Tia just couldn't stop obsessing over Sherise and Ty. And people who teased her about her accent. And teachers who said her last name wrong. And girls who wouldn't sit with her at lunch because her clothes were out of style. Ty wasn't like them before. Would he be that way now? She was spinning in every direction. "I hate this. I hate not being in control!" Tia said out loud.

Nishell opened the bathroom door. "T?" she said.

When Tia saw Nishell, she broke down. She just started bawling about Kiki, Ty, Sherise, and how she'd never get any votes now.

Nishell tried to calm her. "Hey, you gotta get a grip. You ain't gonna make it if you don't chill. You don't want Sherise to see she's got the best of you already, do ya? Especially with Ty. Maybe you need somethin' to take the edge off before you explode."

Tia didn't really know what Nishell was saying. But she did realize she was not in control. That was not good. Tia knew a lot of kids did stuff to relax. Drank, smoked, took pills. She had never thought about doing it herself. Maybe it would make her more like everybody else. That was what she wanted, right?

"You got something like that?" Tia asked.

"Maybe. If you really need it, I'll give it to you. I just don't like seein' you so wound up. You gotta give it a rest, girl. This whole YC thing is makin' you crazy. I saw Ty in the hall. He was walking away from Sherise, tellin' her to drop it."

"He was? I can't believe it," Tia said.

"Obviously," Nishell said. "You don't even see when people are standin' up for you. You got your game focused on one goal: winning. But remember you got friends too. Don't just drop your friends 'cause you wanna win. 'Cause what if you don't? Then what? You gonna jump out the window or somethin'? I know you want to win real bad. But it's not the end of the world if you don't, ya know? You just gotta be you. Be real. If you need somethin' to help you settle a little, maybe it's worth a try. Think about it, okay? Now, we best get movin' or we'll be late," Nishell said.

Nishell gave Tia a lot to think about as they headed into class together. She felt confused. But for now, she'd better just concentrate and not fall behind in school. That would be the last thing she needed. She managed to pay attention until the bell rang at the end of class.

"See you in Mr. Gupta's room after school," Nishell said to Tia. They had different classes the rest of the afternoon. Nishell pressed a pill into Tia's hand. "If you need it," she said.

Tia felt the pill in her pocket all afternoon. It was like a lead weight. It was all she could think about. Should she take it? She'd be like everyone else then. What if her mama found out? Would she get in trouble? Would it make her sick?

Tia decided not to take it. She was strong, like her mama said. She'd do fine without it.

When she met Nishell outside Mr. Gupta's room after the last bell rang, Tia gave the pill back to Nishell.

"I can't," Tia said.

"Keep it," Nishell said, handing it back. "Just in case."

"Tia!" She heard a voice call. She put the pill back in her pocket and turned around. It was Ty.

"Go on in. I'll be there in a minute," Tia told Nishell. Nishell nodded and went into the art room.

Tia looked up at Ty. "You got something to say to me, Ty?" she asked, tapping her foot. Tia wished now she'd taken that pill.

"Tia, I'm sorry," Ty said. "I didn't know you were in yearbook club before. Maybe there's somethin' to it if you like it. I think I'm gonna check it out."

"So?" Tia asked. She was still angry. "I saw you talkin' to Sherise."

"She heard I was thinkin' of joining," Ty said. "She cornered me. I only wanted to check out YC 'cause of you. Come on, Tia. Give me a break. I'll join YC. Just go out with me."

Tia wavered. Her mama didn't want her going on any dates. She'd be grounded forever. But maybe Tia should give Ty a second chance. If he really proved himself, maybe Tia would risk trouble at home for him.

"I'll give you a shot if you're for real," she told him. "Be at the next meeting. Right now, I got a lot of work to do." She quickly opened the art room door and went inside.

Nishell was the only student in the art room. Mr. Gupta always kept the room open. He was super cool. Earlier, Mr. Gupta even said he would sign Tia's detention slip if she came in and worked there.

Nishell raised her eyebrows to ask what happened. Tia mouthed, "Later." Even if Mr. Gupta was cool, she didn't want to talk about what went down with Ty in front of a teacher.

Tia got out her notebook and tried to work on her speech. She'd been thinking about what to say ever since the meeting yesterday. She had all these ideas for how she would make yearbook club rock. She just couldn't think of how to say them the right way. Soon she had a pile of crumpled papers in front of her. She pushed them away and looked around the room. "What's wrong with me?" Tia wondered.

Nishell looked up from the poster she was making for Tia. "How's it goin'?" she asked.

"Not good. I have no words for what I want to say," Tia said.

Tia was starting to panic again. She *had* to show Ms. O her speech on Friday. What if Ms. O said it was awful? Tia wished Nishell could just write it for her. She put her hands in her pockets and felt the pill again. She thought, "Maybe the chill pill would help." But she put that thought right out of her mind again.

Tia's thoughts wandered to other things. Sherise probably hadn't even started her speech. While Tia worked hard, it seemed like Sherise was doing nothing but making the rounds and having a good time, making sure she was in everyone's face.

Nishell came over to her. "How about I take a look?"

Tia smoothed out the last page she had crumpled up. She handed it to Nishell. After reading it, Nishell said, "You've got some cool ideas here, girl. You just need to put them in an order that makes sense."

"How's the campaign going?" Mr. Gupta asked. He was grading an art assignment at his desk. Tia and Nishell looked over at him. "You girls look like you are working hard."

"Tia is havin' some trouble writin' down what she wants to say in her speech," Nishell said.

Mr. Gupta peered over his glasses. "Maybe I can be of some help."

"That would be great, Mr. Gupta," Tia said.

Mr. Gupta thought for a moment. Then he said, "Giving a campaign speech is kind of like applying for a job, right? You want to convince the yearbook club members that you'd be the best person for the job of club president."

"I guess so," Tia said. "I hadn't thought of it that way."

Mr. Gupta continued, "So, what if Nishell asks you questions, like she's interviewing you for a job. You can answer the questions out loud and Nishell can write down what you say. Sometimes talking about things helps you organize your thoughts and ideas."

"Hey, Mr. Gupta, that's a great idea," Nishell said. "What do you think, Tia?"

"Well, I suppose it's worth a try," Tia replied. "For sure, nothing else is working."

Nishell sat at the table across from Tia with the notebook and pen. "So, Tia," she said, "why do you want to be the yearbook club president?"

"I ... I ..." Tia stuttered. "Because I'm crazy," Tia thought to herself.

Then she took a deep breath and tried again. "I want to be YC president because I love yearbook club. Ever since I started school in the United States, I wanted to help make a yearbook. They are really special. They help people remember fun times. The yearbook never came out last year. I want to make sure we put one out this year and that it's the best one ever."

"That's great stuff, Tia," Nishell said, writing quickly in the notebook. Tia felt better all of a sudden. It was easier talking about it than writing it down.

"Okay, next question," Nishell said. "What will you do as president to make the yearbook club better than ever?"

Tia took another deep breath. "I feel we need more members in YC. The more there are, the less work for everyone. That means more fun for everyone too. I have already started working on getting more students to sign up." She knew this was something that Ms. O wanted too.

Tia continued, "Next, I would make sure we work together to get the yearbook out on time, before the end of the school year."

"Nice!" Nishell said. "Last question. What makes you different from the other candidate?"

That question hit Tia like a ton of bricks. How was she supposed to answer that and not become more of a target for teasing? "Don't lose it. Stay cool," Tia thought. Then she cleared her throat.

"Many of you may not know me. I am from Mexico. My family saved money to move to the United States. We came to open a bakery. We still speak Spanish at home a lot. We are proud of our culture. We are also proud to be in America.

"I am a good worker at school and at my family's bakery every day. I want to help make a great yearbook this year. Some say I'm different. I guess I am. But aren't we all in some way? It's no reason to be mean. We need to respect and listen to each other. As YC president, I will make sure everyone gets a say and is included. I want people who might feel left out to join YC. It can be a good place to meet other people, make new friends, share ideas, work, and have fun together. Not just a place to get out of detention. The yearbook should have pictures, events, and stories from everyone. Not just the popular crowd. Please vote for me for YC president."

Mr. Gupta and Nishell both clapped.

"Bravo!" Mr. Gupta said.

"Yeah! You rocked it, girl." Nishell said. She gave the notebook to Tia.

Tia thought she was going to pass out. She actually did it! She got through her speech.

Mr. Gupta said, "Tia, that was perfect! You really have thought about how YC can make a difference. For you and for others. For the school. I know Ms. Okoro will agree."

Tia snapped her fingers. "Nishell, I got it! That will be the theme for my speech. How everyone deserves a chance to fit in and work together."

"I knew you could do it," Nishell said.

Tia was so excited. "Thanks, Nishell. You too, Mr. Gupta. Even if I do not win, everyone will know who I am. What I think. What I feel. Different is good."

Mr. Gupta went back to grading the artwork. "That's what I like to hear," he said with a smile.

Tia started working on her speech again. The notes Nishell had taken while Tia was talking really helped. Now she knew what she wanted to say. Sometimes, if she was lost or didn't know a word, she'd ask Nishell or Mr. Gupta for help. After twenty minutes, her speech was nearly finished.

"Hey, Tia," Nishell said. "Wanna see the poster I made for your campaign? I think it's lookin' pretty sweet."

"*Si!*" Tia smiled. "I bet it will be perfect. You are such a good artist!"

Nishell held up the poster. It was terrific! Tia loved the sparkling words in red, white, and blue. Then they heard a crash over by the door.

[chapter]
6

Tia and Nishell looked around. Marnyke was picking up an easel she'd knocked over. Nishell quickly turned the poster over.

"Hey, girls!" Marnyke said. "I been lookin' for y'all everywhere."

Tia and Nishell looked at each other in confusion. Marnyke didn't talk to either one of them much these days. She was too busy chasing boys or tagging after Sherise.

"What do ya mean?" Nishell asked.

"You guys are missin' all the fun!" Marnyke said. "Us girls in YC are gettin' together after school. We're watchin' the boys' b-ball practice and hangin' out. You in?"

Tia and Nishell looked at each other. What was Marnyke up to?

"I thought you guys knew about it," Marnyke said smugly.

"First I heard," Tia said.

Marnyke laughed. "Girl, you just always got your head in a book. Or somewhere else. I invited you, like, five times yesterday. Maybe you just didn't hear me. Or *understand* me."

Tia felt really brainless. Had Marnyke really invited her to hang out with everyone? Maybe Tia was wrong about Marnyke. Maybe Marnyke was being nice.

Marnyke walked over closer to Tia. She was trying to get a glimpse of Tia's speech. Tia didn't like the way Marnyke was eyeing it. She probably saw all the cross-outs and misspelled words. Tia flipped the paper over.

"What you guys workin' on so hard anyways?" Marnyke asked. "It ain't like there's a huge test tomorrow."

"We're workin' on Tia's speech for YC," Nishell said.

"Oh, really?" Marnyke said, seeming uninterested now. "Cool. So, you guys think a lot of people will join this year?"

"Yeah, I think so. If it's different than it was last year," Nishell said. "Why?"

"Well, I don't know. It's not that cool to be in YC. Mostly a bunch of losers from detention." Marnyke shrugged. "Maybe if it was not so much work all the time and more fun. Maybe it would be cool to be in YC."

Tia got excited. She was thinking pretty much what Marnyke was saying. "I got some ideas how to get others to join YC!" Tia exclaimed.

"Oh, really!" Marnyke said. "You think you can get people to join YC? 'Cause that would be sweet."

Then Tia started reciting her speech again. "Everyone in YC will get a say this year. And be included in everything. Everyone will work together. Then it won't be so much work for just a few. We can all have some fun." Tia said. "This year it will be different and we will get a lot of new members with new ideas and talents. Some people are different. No one ever asks them to be in clubs. If we give everyone a fair shot, we can have an awesome club this year!"

"Yeah? That sounds pretty cool," Marnyke said.

"Thanks!" Tia exclaimed. "I've been working on it with—"

"Marnyke!" Nishell interrupted. "Why do you care so much what Tia's gonna say? I thought you were helpin' Sherise?"

Marnyke was about to answer when her phone buzzed. She quickly checked the screen.

"Gotta dip!" She waved. "Kiki says the boys are back from their run. They're shootin' hoops again."

She ran out of the room. No mention of Tia and Nishell coming with her to join the other girls.

"Oh, no!" Nishell put her head in her hands.

"What?" Tia asked. "Do you want to go watch the boys play basketball? I still have more work to do, but you could go ahead ..."

"No way," Nishell said. "Marnyke is playin' us, girl!"

"What do you mean?" Tia asked.

"She came in here lookin' to spy on you for Sherise. She saw the poster I'm makin'. She tried to read your speech, but you flipped it over. Then she got you to tell her what you are going to say! You watch. Now Sherise will give a speech 'bout having fun and getting more members. She won't have to do nothin' then except yak at everybody, look good, and flirt with the guys. Everyone will want to vote for her!"

Tia felt her eyes well up. "Would Sherise and Marnyke really do that?"

"For sure! You think Marnyke woulda left the boys basketball practice for any other reason? And I never heard her invite you to hang with them yesterday," Nishell added.

Tia couldn't believe Marnyke and Sherise had been plotting against her. "What am I going to do?" Tia cried.

"We'll figure somethin' out. Maybe change your speech?" Nishell suggested. But she didn't look too sure.

"Sounds like you have a bit of a problem, girls. Some dirty politics," Mr.

Gupta said. "Tia, stand your ground. If you change your speech, you're just letting others get the best of you. Besides, it's what you really believe and want. They can't say it like you can say it. You really mean it, and it shows."

Tia nodded. She was trying not to cry. She was feeling like the room was closing in on her. And she wasn't really listening to what Mr. Gupta or Nishell were saying to make her feel better.

"Excuse me. I gotta ... go to the bathroom. I'll be back," Tia said, racing out of the room, not even looking at Nishell.

Tia walked around the school aimlessly, chewing her fingernails. What could she do? Should she really just give her speech now that Marnyke and Sherise knew all about it? She wanted to be YC president, but would she end up being the joke of the school? Tia really wanted to feel like everything she did mattered. Maybe Tia was the only one who felt this way and no one else even cared. So why should she care so much? Maybe the pill could make all of this just go away. Or maybe not. "Forget it," Tia thought, throwing the pill into a trash can. She didn't want that kind of temptation anymore. She wanted to be herself.

Suddenly Tia bumped right into someone. "Sorry!" she muttered and tried to keep walking.

"Tia?" It was Darnell. "Hey girl, what up? You're not lookin' too hot."

Tia wiped the tears off her face. "Nothing. What are you doing here?"

"Basketball. I'm on the team, 'member?" Darnell said. Tia noticed he was wearing his practice uniform.

"Oh, sorry. I wasn't paying attention I guess," Tia said.

"Girl, somethin' is wrong. You gotta tell me," Darnell said.

Tia thought about it. Would Darnell believe her? He hung with Marnyke a lot. Sherise flirted with him all the time too.

"I can't. You won't like it," Tia said.

"What is it, Tia?" Darnell asked again.

"I've been played," Tia blurted out. "Marnyke just came into Mr. Gupta's room where Nishell and I were working on my campaign. She tricked me into telling her what I'm going to say in my speech. Now she'll go tell Sherise. I'll lose. For sure."

"No way, Tia. Marnyke and Sherise wouldn't do that. You got it all wrong," Darnell said.

"I knew you wouldn't believe me!" Tia said.

"No, wait," Darnell said. "I'll get to the bottom of this. Just chill, okay? It'll be all right."

"You will help me?" Tia asked.

"Yeah. We're tight, right? You and me," Darnell said.

"*Si*," Tia answered.

"Well, you got my back in Spanish class. I got your back here. Just be easy. I got this," Darnell said.

Tia nodded.

"Catch ya later," Darnell said as he ran off.

Tia wasn't so sure Darnell would do anything. What if Marnyke or Sherise just played him? Would he still vote for Tia? They might tell him Tia was being crazy. Would he believe them?

Tia walked back to the art room. Mr. Gupta was gone. Nishell had finished the poster. Nishell looked annoyed but sort of worried when she looked at Tia.

"Hey, girl," Nishell said. "It's gettin' late. We're done here today."

Tia nodded. The girls packed up their backpacks and headed for the bus.

"You know you got some great ideas. About includin' everybody who joins YC and workin' as a team," Nishell said.

"Yeah, you're right," Tia said. "But what am I going to do now?"

"Don't worry 'bout it. I think your ideas are ten times better than anything Sherise is gonna come up with. I bet she'll freak out when she finds out what you're gonna say. Plus you already got a bunch of people on your side," Nishell said.

"You think?" Tia asked.

"Yeah," Nishell said confidently. "For sure Ty and me, maybe more. Sherise could even change her mind 'bout running. If you're lucky."

Tia cheered up. Maybe that would happen. Or maybe Sherise would get run over by a bus. Tia knew that wasn't nice, but that's how she felt right now.

When Nishell and Tia got to the bus stop, Nishell's bus showed up first.

"See ya *mañana!*" Nishell said. "Don't worry, *chica*. It'll all work out."

Tia sat on the bench at the bus stop alone. She wondered if she should rewrite her speech or not. Would Ty actually come to a YC meeting? Would Darnell really figure out if Marnyke and Sherise were trying to bring her down?

Tia heard high heels clicking down the sidewalk. It was Marnyke. "Oh, great," Tia thought. Marnyke was coming to wait for the bus too!

Tia was not going to take any more crap today. They weren't friends right now. Marnyke had betrayed Tia. No way was Tia taking the same bus.

"I forgot something," Tia lied. "I'll take the next bus," she muttered as she got up to leave.

"Wait! Tia," Marnyke called. She looked like she'd been crying.

Tia hesitated.

"Tia, I'm sorry," Marnyke said. "I am. Sherise made me spy on you guys. She made me tell her 'bout your speech and everything."

"Yeah, I figured that out," Tia said as she started walking away again.

"Tia, please. I am real sorry," Marnyke said. "I don't know how, but Darnell found out. He called me a two-faced, cheatin' skank. He says he wouldn't ever talk to me again unless I made it right. Please forgive me, you gotta."

"Why should I?" Tia said coldly. It felt good to be mean to Marnyke. She'd hurt Tia a lot. "You spy on me. You are mean. You are trying to ruin my chance to be YC president. How can I forgive you?"

"Look, I said I was sorry. But it's your own fault. I heard you been flirtin' with everyone! Sherise and I saw you flirtin' with Ty outside of class the other day. Then you was flirtin' with Darnell. And

I heard about Jackson. You can't be goin' 'round stealin' men and not expect somethin' back."

Tia's mouth fell open. "Ty? But Sherise was flirting with him too! And I was just being nice to Darnell. We are friends. Only friends!"

"That's what I thought. But Sherise didn't see it that way. She said you had it comin'. But I'll tell you somethin'. Somethin' no one else knows," Marnyke said. "Sherise is real freaked out 'bout your plan. Girl, you got her on the run. She's gonna do somethin' big," Marnyke said.

"Like what?" Tia asked.

Marnyke shrugged. "I dunno yet. Please, are you gonna tell Darnell I apologized? I really like him. I don't know what I'll do if he won't talk to me again."

"I'll think about it," Tia said smugly. "But you have to do something for me. Promise not to help Sherise anymore."

"Promise!" Marnyke cried.

"Okay, I forgive you," Tia said. She didn't feel any better, though. Her head was spinning again. What was the big thing Sherise was scheming? And how could Tia stop Sherise from winning the election?

[chapter]

7

Tia walked in the door in silence. Dinner was on the table. It was *chile rellenos* and *tortillas*. Usually she loved *chile rellenos*. Her mom made them extra big, stuffed with cheese and meat too. Tia could eat four or even five—more than anyone else in the family!

"Sorry I'm late," Tia said. She sat down in her chair. She felt like she was going to throw up. Tia wasn't hungry tonight. She couldn't stop thinking about what Sherise was planning to do to make Tia look bad. What would Sherise do to get everyone on her side?

Tia was in no mood to talk. Luckily for her, the rest of the family had a lot to say. Carlota and Manuel talked about the bakery. They were so busy they might have to hire another worker. Then Tomás wanted to tell Tia all about his day.

"I helped *mami* and *papi* lots today!" Tomás said. "Then I lost my front tooth. See?" He smiled, showing the empty spot where he'd been wiggling his front tooth back and forth all week.

"And I drew a picture. Of you! As *el presidente*!"

Tia tried to smile. She didn't think she'd ever be any kind of president now. "Thanks, Tomás," she said.

"Wait. Let me show you!" He tried to jump out of his seat at the table.

"No," Carlota said. "It is on the fridge. You can show Tia after dinner, *si*?"

"Okay, Mama," Tomás said with a little pout. Tia could see his other front tooth poking out onto his fat lip. He looked like a little old grandfather, an *abuelo* who'd lost all his teeth. It was the funniest thing Tia had seen all day. She giggled.

"Here, *mi hermano*," Tia said lifting another *chile* onto Tomás's plate. "All that hard work deserves an extra *chile*."

"*Gracias*, Tia!" Tomás said, smiling again. The open space in his teeth seemed even funnier now. Tia giggled again.

"*Mi hija*. How was your day? You're so quiet," her dad asked as he finished a bite of *tortilla*.

Tia shrugged. She didn't want to tell them about getting detention, and she *couldn't* tell them anything about Ty. They'd ground her for a month! And telling them about all the backstabbing, scheming, and lies with the election would only worry them.

Tia picked at the *chile* on her plate. She tried to think of something good to say about her day. "It was okay. Nishell and Mr. Gupta, the art teacher, helped me work on my speech. They gave me a lot of good ideas. I think it's almost ready."

"That sounds good!" Carlota said, serving everyone another *tortilla*. Tia's stomach grumbled. She couldn't handle eating any more.

Tia felt her phone buzz in her pocket. Was it Ty? Or was it Marnyke with more info on Sherise's surprise? Was it Nishell with a new idea for Tia's speech? It could even be Darnell, saying he'd figured everything out.

Tia had to know who it was. Her parents never let her check her phone at the table, though. She had to get away.

"May I be excused, please? I'd like to finish working on my speech," Tia asked quickly.

Tia saw her mom shoot a look at her father. Usually leaving the dinner table during a meal was not allowed. Dinner was family time in Tia's house. No TV, no homework, no cell phones. For a second, Tia thought they were going to say no.

"Go on," Carlota said slowly. "But be back to help wash up."

Tia didn't need to be told twice. She got up quickly. When she was out of the dining room, she pulled her phone out of her pocket.

Her screen flashed. The text wasn't Ty, Darnell, Marnyke, or Nishell. It was from Kiki! "Hey T. I know u r mad I wouldn't help w/the campaign. But Reesie sez u don't need me. Got lots of help. Sry. Still friends?"

Tia wanted to cry again. She wasn't sure she could forgive Kiki. Just because she found other people to help didn't mean Kiki's refusal didn't still hurt.

Tia didn't text her back. "Why should I bother to even respond?" she thought. Tia wished Kiki could just be true to her friends, and not be pushed around by her sister.

Tia went upstairs to get a grip. She had to get her mind off the day. She decided to do some research for her history paper due next week. It was on the Mexican–American War of 1846. She turned on the computer, but she was too distracted to study. She decided to check her e-mail and Facebook page.

Some friends back in Mexico had posted some messages! Tia smiled. She was so happy to get some friendly news instead of all the mean gossip. Her friends wanted to know what she was up to. They hadn't heard from Tia in a while. She must be making all new friends. Having too much fun. Her friend Raul even asked when she was coming back to visit.

Tia started to feel much better. She checked the Facebook status of a few other people. Then Tia looked at Sherise's page. Would she be posting about the election?

To Tia's surprise, Sherise had posted an invite to a party. "Friday Nite @ 10!" it said. Tia clicked on the party link. On top was a picture of a smiling Sherise. Next to her was a poster that looked just like the one Nishell had made for Tia. It was red, white, and blue. It read. "DON'T BE A FOOL!!! MAKE YC COOL! VOTE SHERISE FOR YC PRESIDENT!!!" Then underneath was a message:

> For all my peeps! I'm throwin' a YC party. Come if you want to have a fun year in YC. BYOB. Pizza and fun are on ME. 10 p.m. Be there! VOTE SHERISE for YC president on Monday. We gonna Kill it!

Sherise and Tia were going to give their speeches on Friday. Then on Monday everyone was going to vote for the new YC president. Even if Tia's speech was better, everyone would be partying at Sherise's that night. What a way to get everyone to vote for her—bribing them with pizza. Sherise was a real piece of work.

Tia also noticed the message said BYOB. There would be drinking too. Tia didn't know how to feel about that. She scrolled down to see who responded. Almost everyone in YC said they were coming. Including Ty! Tia hadn't been invited. Tia called Nishell.

"What up, girl?" Nishell answered.

"Were you invited to Sherise's party?" Tia asked.

There was a short pause. "Yeah, I was. But I ain't said nothin' yet. I don't know if I'm gonna go," Nishell said.

"Why would you do that to me?" Tia asked. She was really upset. "I thought you were on my side."

"Yeah, but I could go and spy or whatever. Like they did," Nishell said. "Didn't you hear? The twins' 'rents are out of town. Good timing, huh? Sherise would *never* be able to do this if they were home. She's gonna go wild. I can hang out. Especially since everybody will be wasted. I'll be able to talk people outta votin' for Sherise."

Nishell had a good point. It wasn't like Tia could just show up at the party and rally for votes herself. She wasn't even invited.

Tia wondered what she'd do Friday night instead. Everyone would be at Sherise's having fun. Except her. Tia would be stuck home alone with no friends and no fun. Ty would probably find a new girl too.

"But ..." Nishell said. "Maybe it's better for me not to go at all, ya know? I mean, if I went it might be too obvious if I was braggin' on you for YC president. For sure Sherise is gonna be all over Darnell and Ty to get their votes. That will piss Jackson off ... so maybe that will be an easy vote for you. Plus, I bet Misha and Tara will vote for you too. Even if they go to the party. They know how Sherise operates. Lots of people do."

Tia bit her fingernail. What was the right thing to do? Go after everyone like Sherise did? Or let Sherise dig her own grave? "Let me know tomorrow what you decide, okay?" Tia said. She hung up the phone.

Tia didn't want to listen to Nishell debate whether or not to go when Tia hadn't even been invited. Tia knew Nishell was trying to be a good friend at least. Not like Kiki. Tia wanted to go to the party too. Usually she was invited. But not this time. She knew Nishell would probably go. Nishell wanted to be in with the popular crowd. All the cool people would be there.

Tia sighed and turned off her computer. She felt really down. There was nothing Tia could do. On Friday, she'd read her speech. She would give it her best. Tia knew what YC needed. A president who worked hard and made sure everyone worked together. Not someone who threw parties and used the fun factor just to win votes. Tia fell asleep wondering if her way would work.

[chapter]

8

Friday morning before school, Tia walked down the hallway to Ms. Okoro's room. Tia was feeling pretty good after a few hours in the bakery pounding dough. Ms. O wanted to hear the speeches Sherise and Tia were giving before the meeting this afternoon.

Surprise! Sherise was already in the room. She looked Tia up and down. "I'm first," she said, staring at Tia's hands.

Tia squirmed. She looked down at her hands. They still had flecks of dough stuck to them from the bakery. She had washed before leaving for school, but it hadn't all come off. She tried brushing it away, but it didn't work.

Ms. Okoro walked in. "Good morning, girls," she said.

Tia let Sherise take the lead. "Hi, Ms. O!" Sherise smiled and jumped up. "We didn't want to waste too much of your time. Tia and I already decided whose going to meet with you first. And I'm ready to start whenever you are!"

Ms. O blinked. "Okay then. Why don't you sit back down and we can get started. Tia, would you mind waiting out in the hall?"

Tia shook her head no and walked out of the room. She didn't want to object. It would sound like she was complaining.

Tia stood in the hallway while Ms. O and Sherise chitchatted. She wondered if she should move but decided to listen. It wasn't like Sherise hadn't already done the same to Tia.

"OMG!" Sherise said excitedly. "Ms. O, I love your necklace with all the wooden beads. My mom has one just like it. I'm always asking her to borrow it."

"Why thank you, Sherise," Ms. O said. "I just bought it last week. This is the first time I've worn it."

"You know, it goes great with everything too. My mom wears hers all the time. I really love it with your yellow shirt. It's totally in."

"Well, thanks again, Sherise. That's nice to hear," Ms. O said.

Tia rolled her eyes. Sherise was completely sucking up to Ms. O! And Ms. O was falling for it.

"Yeah. No prob, Ms. O. So anyway, here's my speech." Tia could hear Sherise handing over a sheet of paper.

There was a brief pause. Then Ms. Okoro said, "Hmmm. This speech is quite short, Sherise. Only a few sentences. Is this really all you plan to say this afternoon?"

"Oh no," Sherise said. "I'm way better at speaking on the fly. Like off-the-cuff. I've got tons of things to say. But I didn't want to put the wrong thing down on paper and be stuck reading it, you know? 'Cause as president I'd have to think on my feet not paper."

"Well, that's a start," Ms. O said. "What about your campaign? What are you planning? How has it been going?"

"Great! Everybody has been very helpful so far. I think everybody just wants what's best for the club," Sherise said. "I can't wait for the election on Monday."

Tia heard Sherise's chair scrape the floor as she stood up. Sherise hadn't really even answered any of Ms. O's questions. And it seemed like Sherise hadn't even written her speech yet. Tia couldn't believe Ms. O was letting her off so easy.

"Later, Ms. O!" Sherise said and walked out the door. She looked Tia right in the eye. "See ya, *chi-ca*. Next time you eavesdrop, try to be a little less obvious," she whispered as she stalked off.

Tia felt anxious and nervous. This was getting so nasty. It could destroy a lot of friendships and even the yearbook club. "I gotta make sure I win. That way I can fix all this," Tia thought.

Ms. Okoro popped her head out of the door. She instantly saw the panicked look on Tia's face. "Tia, come right in," she said with a soothing smile. Tia sat down across the table from her. "So how are you coming along?" Ms. Okoro asked.

"Um. Fine," Tia said. She wanted Ms. O to think that she was doing well. She didn't want to sound like a whiner. And she didn't want to rat on Sherise for being so mean. But Tia just couldn't be as bubbly and fake as Sherise right now.

Tia pulled out her speech. She'd rewritten it on fresh paper to make it look nice for Ms. O. "Here's what I am going to say this afternoon."

Ms. O read the speech. It was almost two full pages. It didn't matter what Sherise's plan was. Tia knew that she'd come up with her ideas all on her own. They were good too.

"You have a lot to say here," Ms. O said. "I really like the part about how you want to encourage new members to join. And about working hard as a team and having fun. Talking about making memories together is good too. You have some really great ideas, Tia."

"Thanks," Tia smiled. She was very proud of her speech. No matter what happened.

"I heard you had some trouble the other day in Mr. Gupta's room. Do you want to talk about it?" Ms. O asked.

Tia didn't know what to say. How much did Ms. O know? "I was there with Nishell working on my speech," Tia said.

"Yes, but is there something else?" Ms. Okoro asked. "I talked to Mr. Gupta yesterday. He said something about how you and Nishell were worried about your ideas being stolen? It sounded like you were accusing Marnyke of spying on your plans. Maybe for Sherise?"

Tia thought fast. "Everything is okay. I have my speech. I am happy with it. I will be glad when the election is over on Monday."

"Are you sure?" Ms. O asked. "Is there anything going on I should know about?"

Tia wanted to tell Ms. O everything. That Marnyke was spying for Sherise. Marnyke had even admitted it! Even worse, Sherise was up to no good with her sneaky party tactics.

But Tia realized Ms. O would have to tell Principal Olson about the party, and then he would put a stop to it. And Tia was the only one who would snitch. No one else had a reason to. They would all know it was her and be mad if she told. Even Nishell. It would spoil all the fun. No one would talk to her ever again. It's one more thing that would make her a target. Tia's mind was racing. She found herself chewing her fingernails.

"Nothing you can help with, really," Tia said and shrugged.

Ms. O didn't seem convinced. Maybe she wasn't fooled by Sherise. It didn't matter, though. Tia wasn't saying a word. The bell rang, saving Tia from having to explain anything more.

"I have to go, Ms. O," Tia said. "I don't want to be tardy to first period."

Tia picked up her backpack. She rushed out the door before Ms. O could ask any more questions.

Out in the hall, Tia stopped short when she saw Marnyke by the door. She had probably listened in to see if Tia was ratting on everyone.

"Marnyke," Tia said. She kept walking.

"Tia, wait." Marnyke ran to catch up with her. "Have you talked to Darnell yet? You promised you would."

Tia shrugged. "I haven't had a chance."

"Well, do it okay?" Marnyke insisted. "'Cause somehow Sherise got him to think it wasn't her fault I was spying. And I don't want her all over my man."

"Fine. I will say something to him in class after lunch," Tia snapped.

Marnyke shook her head. "Thanks, Tia. I know we're not great friends or whatever, but at least *you're* honest. You might use people, but you don't stab them in the back. And you know what? If you do this for me, you got my vote. But don't tell anyone. Or I'll make you pay."

Marnyke walked off without another word. Was being honest and real better than winning? Tia wasn't sure. She didn't feel very honest right now. Especially after lying to Ms. O.

"*Hola! Chica!*" Nishell's fingers snapped in front of Tia's face. "You home in there?"

"What? Sorry. I was thinking," Tia replied.

"I bet. I saw you talkin' to Marnyke. Were you bitchin' her out for spyin'?"

Tia shook her head. She forgot she had never told Nishell about seeing Marnyke at the bus stop. Tia wasn't going to tell Nishell now. She didn't want Marnyke to hear about it later. There was already enough gossip going around at this school.

"I told her if she and Sherise try anything else, I'd bust a cap in their asses," Tia bluffed.

Nishell smiled and high-fived her. "Way to go, sista. I'll make you a badass yet!"

Tia gave a small smile. She felt even worse for lying to Nishell now. Tia wasn't honest like Marnyke said.

"Oh and I've decided," Nishell said. "We're gonna have a girls' night tonight. Jus' you and me. It'll be tight. We'll have movies and popcorn."

"Oh! That sounds perfect!" Tia said. At least she'd have something to look forward to other than thinking about the election. And the party she was not invited to. And what Ty was doing at the party. "Thanks, Nishell. You're the best."

"My mom is working the night shift," Nishell said. "No adults! We could have a real party of our own."

Tia wasn't so sure. What was Nishell really talking about? Drinking? Like at Sherise's party? Tia didn't know if she was up for that right now. She had enough pressure from everything else that was spinning in her head.

"That's cool!" Tia faked another smile. Maybe Nishell would forget about it. At least Tia wouldn't be all by herself.

"Gotta head to class. Check ya later," Nishell said, walking away.

Tia was heading to her first class when she spotted Darnell. It was now or never. Tia took a deep breath.

"*Hola*, Darnell," Tia said. "We gotta talk."

"I know," Darnell said. "Turns out Marnyke was doin' everythin' on her own. Sherise said she didn't have nothin' to do with puttin' Marnyke up to it."

"Darnell, Marnyke apologized to me for spying and I forgave her. She wanted

—

you to know," Tia forced out. "She and I are all square now."

"For real?" One of Darnell's eyebrows went up. "You an' Marnyke? Especially when you guys ain't ever been that tight in the first place."

"Hey, at least Marnyke said she was sorry," Tia told him.

The bell rang. Class was starting.

"I gotta go," Tia said. "But I'm being straight with you. Marnyke and I, we're cool. Give her a break. Just watch your back with Sherise, okay?"

Tia walked away before Darnell could say anything else. She had kept her word and done what she promised Marnyke. At least she had Marnyke on her side now. Supposedly.

But would it be enough to win the election?

—

[chapter]

9

What a day! Tia collapsed on the couch. She couldn't believe all that had happened, and there was still more to go. And she still had to help at the bakery, pack, and head over to Nishell's for their girls' night!

Her mom wandered into the living room. She saw Tia lying on the couch.

"Tia!" she cried. "How did your speech go? What happened at the meeting? Tell me everything. You can't leave until I hear it all."

"Okay, okay," Tia said. "Nishell and I got to the meeting early. We hung my

—

poster in the front of the room. Mama, it looked *so* good! It was sparkly and had pictures and was really cool. Everyone saw it when they came in. They all started talking about it."

"And what about the other candidates?" her mother asked. "How did they do?"

"Sherise is the only other candidate. Her poster wasn't as good as mine," Tia said proudly. She had to thank Nishell again for all her hard work.

"What else?" her mom said.

"Well, a lot of new people showed up. Even cousin Mario was there. We almost didn't have seats for everyone," Tia continued.

Tia smiled as she thought about how Ty had been there too. The whole day she'd been worried he wouldn't come. Then, there he was, sitting in the back, right next to Darnell and Jackson. Afterward he even asked her out on Saturday. But Tia wasn't going to tell her mom that.

"Ms. O was surprised by the turnout. She wasn't expecting such a crowd. Ms. O even said she thought they would have the best YC year ever," Tia explained.

Tia told her mama about how she had talked to a lot of people in her classes about YC. How it would be different and better this year. There were kids that Tia didn't know there too. The buzz was out. Tia had heard almost everybody whispering about Sherise's party. But Tia decided to leave those details out too.

"Sherise gave her speech first," Tia said. "Her speech was all about having fun. She said she had more experience because she'd been at the school longer than me. A lot of people cheered at that. Sherise promised to make sure they'd get work done just as long as they had fun doing it."

"It was pretty good," Tia told her mom. "It didn't last very long, though. It was only two minutes.

"Then it was my turn," Tia said. "I read my whole speech. I did really good, Mama. I talked about giving everyone a chance to work together as a team. We would work hard. I told them we would do fun things too. I even added something I thought of just today. Trying to win the state yearbook competition this year."

"Oh that's really good!" her mom exclaimed.

Tia smiled. A few people had snickered when Tia talked about working hard, but Nishell stood up for her. She glared at anyone who wasn't quiet while Tia was talking. At the end of Tia's speech, she'd seen people nodding at her suggestions too. Even Ty seemed impressed. That's when he came up to her and asked her out.

"Well, it sounds like you did really well," Carlota said. "Whatever happens, you know that your *papi* and I are very proud of you."

She gave Tia a hug. "*Gracias*, Mama," Tia said.

"Now go. Have some fun with your friend!" Carlota said. "You worked so hard this week. At school and at the bakery. You can have the night off. Your father and I can handle it. Who knows, maybe we'll even call in Mario to help."

"Really, Mama?" Tia exclaimed.

"*Si*! Go. Before I change my mind!" Carlota joked.

Tia rushed up the stairs to call Nishell and tell her she could come early. They might even have time for two movies!

As Tia packed her overnight bag, her mind drifted to the election. Tia knew she'd done her best. She told everyone she would work hard to make YC the best club it could be. Sherise had only talked about fun and what that meant to her.

Tia also knew that almost all of the new people were going to Sherise's tonight. Who would everyone really vote for?

The TV screen dimmed as the first movie ended.

"What do you wanna do now?" Nishell asked, taking another handful of popcorn.

"I really liked it," Tia said. "Could we watch another?"

Tia was exhausted. She almost fell asleep during the movie. But thoughts of Sherise's party crept into her head. Ty was probably there. And Marnyke. She wondered what they were doing. Tia really just wanted to go to sleep and forget the whole thing. But she didn't want to disappoint Nishell.

"Nah," Nishell said. "We gotta do somethin' we'll remember. Somethin' cool. Otherwise we're just gonna end up feeling lame while everybody else is havin' fun."

Tia knew she meant Sherise's party. "Do you wish you were at Sherise's?" Tia asked.

"No, I really don't, Tia. Hey! I just got an idea. Hold on." Nishell got up and walked out of the room.

By the time Tia stood up, Nishell was back with something in her hands. It was a pack of cigarettes.

"Come on. Let's hit the porch," Nishell said.

They went out and sat on the steps. Nishell opened the pack. She took out a cigarette and lit it. "Here." She tossed the pack to Tia.

"Nishell!" Tia exclaimed. "What if your mom finds out?"

"She's not gonna find out unless you tell her. She's workin' and my bro is sleepin' at a friend's. Have a smoke and chill. You can't always be so uptight, girl."

Tia blushed. Did everyone think she was such a goody two-shoes? Was it because she never smoked or drank? Or took pills? She was gonna prove everyone wrong. She could be cool too.

Tia took out a cigarette and held it out for Nishell to light.

Nishell lit Tia's cigarette. Then Nishell pulled out her phone. "We should see what's goin' down at that party."

Tia took a puff of the cigarette and coughed in surprise. It hurt!

"No, no. I didn't mean go over there!" Nishell said, misunderstanding Tia's cough. "I'm just gonna text a few people."

Tia didn't try to change Nishell's mind. Tia didn't want Nishell to know that this was the first cigarette she'd ever tried.

—

"You can text people too," Nishell said.

Tia knew Nishell just wanted to see what was going on with Jackson. She'd been talking about how much she liked him all night long. Nishell's phone buzzed.

"OMG! Looks like Darnell has gone wacko! Misha said he broke his phone throwin' it against a wall!" Nishell said.

Tia hoped that wasn't true. She decided to be brave and text Jackson. Maybe he would tell her something about Ty. **"Hey. How's the party?"**

"Man. It's crazy here! Everyone is wasted!" Jackson texted back.

Tia didn't know what to say to that. Then, right away she got two more texts from Jackson.

Tia looked at the first one and gasped. **"Just kissed Sherise. Oops. Bad me."**

Nishell heard Tia's gasp. "What?" Nishell asked. "Who texted you?"

Tia looked at her second message. "DON'T Tell Nishell! SWEAR. Or we ain't friends no more."

Tia didn't want to lose a friend. Plus Nishell would only get hurt. Tia texted back, "K."

"For real, what text did you just get?" Nishell asked.

"I ... uh ... it just sounds like everybody is drinking and having fun at Sherise's party," Tia said.

"Well, let's have a little more fun of our own," Nishell suggested. She ran inside and came back out with some beers. "Come on. It's no big deal."

"I don't know ..." Tia said. This was worse than smoking.

"Are you gonna be lame or are you gonna be cool?" Nishell asked, taking a swig.

Tia looked at the beer. She wasn't going to be lame. She wasn't. And why not drink some? Everyone else was having fun already. Why not Tia too?

Tia opened her beer and took a long drink.

"That's my home girl," Nishell said.

They raced to see who could finish their beer the fastest. It was okay with Tia because the beer tasted horrible. She just wanted to get it over with. After they finished, Tia felt a little light-headed.

"Have another," Nishell said. She handed another can to Tia. Tia took a drink.

"Jackson is so fine," Nishell sighed. "His eyes. I mean, come on!"

Tia shrugged. "Forget about him, Nishell. He ain't what you think." Nishell had been talking about Jackson all night. Tia wondered if Ty was kissing girls too. Just like Jackson.

"I can't! Plus he's been flirtin' with me! Did I tell you he let me borrow his jacket last week when I was freezing? How sweet was that?"

Tia felt horrible. She couldn't let Nishell go on like this. "Jackson kissed Sherise at the party!" she blurted out.

"What?" Nishell wailed. She started to cry. "I've been hot on him for a while. Sherise knows it too. It's not fair! How could he kiss Sherise now?"

"I don't know," Tia said. "I'm sorry."

"He asked me out to a movie next week. Maybe he forgot. I shoulda gone to that party. I shoulda known better," Nishell said, sniffling. "I jus' can't believe it. Where is Darnell? 'Cause you know Sherise was all over him too."

"I don't know. I wasn't supposed to tell you though," Tia said. "You can't say anything, Nishell. I don't need any more trouble. I already got enough. Okay?"

Nishell nodded. Tia's head was spinning. How would she get out of this?

—

[chapter]

10

Ms. Okoro said, "I have counted the votes, and ..." she paused. Tia could hardly sit still. She'd waited all weekend for this. She could barely get any homework done on Sunday. All she could think of was the election and Ty. Ty had texted her on Saturday saying he couldn't hang with her. He didn't even give a reason. Tia was mad. Did he care more about the party than hanging with her? She didn't know what to say back. So she just didn't reply.

Nishell wasn't any help. She'd called Tia every fifteen minutes on Sunday to talk about what a sleezeball Jackson was. Then she said she wasn't going out with him on Friday, even though she still really wanted to. At the end of every conversation, Nishell convinced herself to go on the date again. By the fifth call, Tia was ready to scream.

Today wasn't any better. Twice, Tia got snapped at by teachers for not paying attention in class. Sherise wasn't doing very well either. She wasn't even wearing one of her matching outfits today. At lunch, someone said Marnyke and Sherise had a blowout Friday night. And Darnell found out the truth about how Sherise was playing Marnyke and Tia. That's why he got so angry he smashed his phone.

At the YC meeting, it looked like it was all true. Darnell and Marnyke were sitting on one side of the room, and Sherise, Kiki, and Jackson were on the other. Ty was in the back corner with his head down. Nobody would even look at Nishell and Tia.

"The winner is ..." Ms. O continued, building the suspense, "Sherise Butler!" Lots of people in the room cheered and hollered. Many looked stunned.

Tia sunk down in her chair. She wanted to cry. All that hard work. All that agony. Wasted. Because Sherise did anything to win.

Sherise stood up in the front of the room. "I'd like to thank everyone who voted for me. We're gonna have a great year, guys! I have so many things planned ... I can't wait to have tons of fun with you all!" Sherise gave a thumbs-up. She walked to the back of the room.

"Thank you, Sherise," Ms. O said. "And congratulations. Everybody worked hard for this. It was a very close race. In fact, only two votes separated the two candidates. Tia has some great ideas. I know Sherise and Tia can work together to help get a lot done. Now let's celebrate! I brought chips and drinks."

More people cheered. Almost everyone was in a good mood.

Lots of people walked over to Sherise right away to congratulate her. She was surrounded. No one even looked at Tia and Nishell.

Nishell went to take Tia's poster down. Tia watched the glitter fall on the floor as Nishell struggled with it. She wished it could've just stayed up there. At least her poster was better than Sherise's.

Tia watched Darnell walk over and help Nishell. Nishell smiled up at him. It was the first time Tia had seen her happy all day long. Darnell was smiling back too!

Tia turned to see Jackson watching the two of them. Tia shrugged. Nishell still hadn't turned Jackson down yet for their date, but she definitely liked the attention from Darnell. Jackson was in deep trouble for two-timing with Sherise. Tia heard after the kiss, Darnell wouldn't talk to Jackson or Sherise. Maybe Darnell was tryin' to one-up Jackson by flirting with a girl Jackson liked. Tia wondered what Marnyke would do now. She was the one who was really into Darnell.

Tia turned around to see Marnyke and Sherise hugging and making up. Guess their fight was over. Didn't look to Tia like Darnell had changed his mind about being mad at Sherise, though. That might be why he was hanging with Nishell. Tia didn't want anyone to get hurt again.

Ty walked up to Tia. "Hey, girl. I'm real sorry about us not hangin' out."

Tia shook her head. "What's up with you, Ty? First you're all about me, then you ditch for no reason? I'm not even gonna mention the party."

"Hey, *chica*." Ty grabbed her hand. Tia's heart started to race. "You know it's always been about you! I only went to the party to watch out for my man D. After he threw the phone, I knew I had to get him home. I broke curfew, and my dad caught me. I'm grounded for life practically. I'll even be in trouble for coming to YC today."

Tia knew Ty was telling the truth. She really liked him too. "Well, how am I ever gonna see you?" she asked.

Ty gave her a crooked smile. "I'm still allowed to go buy groceries. You better bet I'll be eating so much bread that I'll have to be at the bakery every day."

Tia blushed and smiled. Ty looked around to see that no one was watching them. Then he gave her a long, soft kiss. Tia was too stunned to say anything.

"Gotta run before my dad realizes somethin' is up. See you 'round, *chica*."

He left before Tia could say anything. Ty really liked her! And he'd come to the bakery just to see her. Maybe she could convince her mama he wasn't so bad.

Tia stood alone for a few minutes watching Sherise, who was surrounded by her admirers. Sherise saw her looking and walked over. Was Sherise going to rub her nose in it?

"No hard feelings?" Sherise asked. She offered Tia her hand.

Tia paused. It could be a trick. Sherise wouldn't even meet Tia's eyes. "Fine," Tia said. She shook Sherise's hand, hard. Sherise pulled her hand away, wincing. Tia smirked. Tia's hands were strong from working in the bakery.

Sherise frowned at Tia. Then she turned around and walked back to her group without saying anything.

Nishell came over and set the poster down. "We did a great job," Nishell said, looking at it proudly.

"I know," Tia sighed. "Thanks for all your help."

"No prob'," Nishell said. She watched Sherise laughing. "What were you and Sherise talking about?"

Tia snorted. "Sherise wants no hard feelings."

"You really think we're gonna have 'tons of fun'?" Nishell asked.

"I don't know," Tia said.

"You think you're gonna forget all the scheming and lies?" Nishell asked.

"Maybe." Tia thought of the hand-shake she just gave Sherise. Sherise had spied, lied, and partied her way to winning. But was Tia really any different? She had tried just as hard to win.

"I just can't believe Jackson." Nishell sent a glare in his direction. "And I can't believe nobody told me what was going on either. You're my only real friend, Tia."

Tia watched Jackson laughing and joking with Sherise across the room. Even Darnell had walked over there to stand with the group. Looked like he didn't want to be left out either. Not like Tia and Nishell were right now.

Tia took a deep breath. She thought of all the nastiness, even her own mean tactics just now with Sherise. Was that really the way she wanted to be? Alone and angry? She couldn't stay mad all year. After all, they were going be stuck together in class and in YC.

"We have to put it all behind us," Tia said. "The election was unfair. We should have won."

"Yeah," Nishell agreed angrily.

Tia turned to Nishell. "But we have to suck it up and join the group. Be a team. Who knows? Maybe it'll get better now."

"Okay, Pollyanna," Nishell muttered.

Tia grabbed Nishell's arm. "We're going over there. You and me. Come on." She pulled Nishell along with her as she walked over to the group around Sherise.

"Sherise," Tia said. "You did a great job. I bet we'll have a great year with you as president."

Sherise looked confused, but smiled. "Thanks?" she said uncertainly.

Tia gave her a genuine smile. Sherise's smile got bigger. Maybe they could work this out.

"Hey, this will be great," Jackson said. "We got a real team goin' here!" He started listing off everyone's roles. "Sherise the leader. Darnell the man. Marnyke the schemer. Kiki the brain. Tia the worker. Nishell the artist. And me!"

He flashed a huge smile at everyone. Marnyke smirked. Nishell raised her eyebrows. Tia just shook her head. What a player Jackson was. Would he ever change?

"And what do you do?" Sherise teased.

"I'll be da face." He smiled at Nishell and winked.

Tia could see Nishell struggling not to show her anger. Tia hoped Nishell wouldn't blurt everything out. Nishell gave a weak smile back at Jackson. Tia sighed with relief.

"You know, Tia," Sherise said. "Jackson's got a point for once. You really work hard. I thought your speech was great. For real."

Tia smiled. She was proud of her speech, even if she didn't win. "Thanks, Sherise."

"I'll really want your help this year, Tia. Maybe we could put some of your ideas into action together! Like making sure everyone has a chance to contribute. It would be cool to make it to the yearbook state competition. Maybe you should be, like, YC manager!"

"For real?" Tia asked. YC manager sounded official to Tia.

"Yeah!" Sherise said. "And we'll have fun too. Right, Nishell?" Sherise turned to Nishell.

Nishell didn't want to look at Sherise though. She was still pretty hot over the whole scene. But Nishell nodded.

"Well, I'm glad of one thing," Kiki interrupted. "That this election is o-v-e-r. The rest of the year will be a piece of cake compared to the last week. I don't wanna have to choose between my sister and one of my friends ever again. Now that it's done we can all be friends and hang out again."

Nishell rolled her eyes. Marnyke snickered.

Tia thought about everything she'd been through. The backstabbing. The fighting. The lying. The stress. The partying. The broken hearts. The ruined friendships.

Tia decided losing friends was the worst. More than anything, she was glad it was over too. And it was good to be happy. Happy about making new friends. About Ty. Maybe some people would never be friends again. But at least they could try.

Tia smiled. It was time to turn over a new leaf. Time to fit in.

"You know what, Kiki? I'd like that. I'd like that a lot."

—